J

THE ONGOING ADVENTURES OF
JERAMIE & MAX

Written
by Roman Neubacher

Illustrated by Gerda Neubacher

Copyright © 1988 by Hayes Publishing Ltd.

ISBN 0-88625-202-4

CHP BOOKS

3312 Mainway, Burlington, Ontario L7M 1A7, Canada
2045 Niagara Falls Blvd., Unit 14, Niagara Falls, NY 14304, U.S.A

Printed in Hong Kong

THE ONGOING ADVENTURES OF
JERAMIE & MAX

Sundays were usually Jeramie's favorite day of the week. No school, no chores and no homework. Today, however, it was raining — a dull gray drizzle that seemed to go on forever. Jeramie sat looking out at the soggy grass, wishing it would dry up. On a rainy day like this, there was never anything to do.

In the family room Max slumped drowsily on his pillow. He glanced around the room at his rubber ball, chewy bones and stale dog food. None were very interesting. Max rolled over onto his back and pretended to play dead, his four paws pointed upward to the ceiling. Jeramie came wandering in and plopped himself down next to Max, saying in a dreary tone, "Well, Max old buddy, nothing's going on."

It was a humdrum Sunday. Jeramie had played all of his video games, but they were no fun. He could easily beat the high score. Max watched but was hardly excited by any of it. Suddenly there was a tremendous crash and bump overhead. Jeramie's mother rushed upstairs, thinking that a painting had fallen off the wall. She came back moments later and reported that all was normal. "Oh, well," she said, "it must have come from the attic."

"Nonsense, honey, the attic's empty. It's just the house settling," replied Dad from behind the paper. "THE ATTIC!" Jeramie's and Max's eyes lit up at the same time. They had never been in the attic.

Jeramie and Max looked all over the house for an opening to the attic, but couldn't find one. It seemed hopeless. Then Jeramie remembered a small door in his closet. He had seen it a long time ago when he helped his father wallpaper his room. They raced to the closet, shoving boxes of shoes, sweaters and jeans, toys and games. Whatever came in their way was tossed aside in the rush to find the secret door. Jeramie felt around the walls, but couldn't find the opening. Huddled in the small closet with Max, he tried to listen for whistling wind, hollow knocking, anything.

Max, with his nose, sniffed at a crack where musty smells were creeping through. As he started to scratch at the wallpaper, Jeramie felt along the lower corner of the closet. Sure enough, there it was.

There was no handle, no sign of hinges; only a faint square outline underneath layers of wallpaper. Jeramie took out his pocketknife. He carefully opened it and slowly cut around the square. Max watched excitedly, thinking, "Wow, this is great! But if Mom catches him, boy will he be in trouble!"

The cutting was done. Jeramie used a wire coat hanger to pry open the door.

There it was! Dark, cold and dusty, smelling of limestone, dampness and stale boards — the attic that nobody had seen for a long, long time. With a flashlight, and his best friend Max, Jeramie ventured slowly up the dark, smelly stairs. Both their hearts were pounding as they moved, step after cautious step, past scattered pieces of broken wood and glass. The glass prompted Jeramie to pick up Max so he wouldn't cut his paws. At the top of the stairs Jeramie shone his light about. There was nothing but scattered old newspapers, chips of wood and lots of dust.

In the middle of the room stood a trunk. It was about as big as a refrigerator, with fancy old strappings covering its brown leather surface. Jeramie brushed off the dust with his sleeve, trying to find some kind of markings.

"I wonder why the people who lived here before didn't take this trunk with them? I wonder what's inside?" he whispered to Max.

"Jewels," thought Max.

"A treasure map," thought Jeramie.

"Old toys!" thought Max, expressing his curiosity with a happy growl.

"Neat old clothes!" whispered Jeramie.

"Old pictures!" barked Max.

Jeramie froze in terror, "or...maybe...a...DEAD BODY!!!"

"AAAAAAGGGGGGHHHHHH!!!" Jeramie screamed, scooped up Max and started to run out of the room. Just then the trunk began to quiver. Jeramie and Max stood there in horror.

The lid began to open, just like it did in old vampire movies. Neither of our two heroes could move a muscle. Their throats were frozen. Not a sound could be heard but the creaking of the chest. The lid opened farther, and a bright light burst from inside, lighting up the room. They stood and watched, wide-eyed, and very, very scared.

The chest now stood open, with light pouring out of it, warming the cold space. Max struggled loose and ran to the trunk, barking. Jeramie went after him. As they stared, a hat emerged from inside, then a head, then a fat little belly, chubby arms, and short, squat legs. The stranger in the trunk had obviously not seen them because the shriek of surprise he let out made Max and Jeramie scream too.

"What are you screaming for?" yelled the little old man.

"Why are you screaming?" Jeramie yelled back.

"Because you startled me!" exclaimed the little man.

"Oh...I'm...I'm very sorry," apologized Jeramie.

"That's alright, but don't sneak up on people," said the old man, and he hopped out of the trunk.

"Who are you?" asked Jeramie, realizing that the stranger was no bigger than he.

"My name is Cerberus the Great," exclaimed the little man with excitement.

"Oh, well, I'm Jeramie, and this is my dog Max."

"Pleased to meet you, Jeramie, and you too, Max," beamed Cerberus.

"How did you get into that trunk?" Jeramie asked cautiously. He still wasn't sure about this whole situation. Max, however, seemed to like Cerberus.

"Well, sit down here and I will tell you." With a snap of his fingers a colorful blanket appeared. Jeramie and Max sat down in amazement. Cerberus told them about a good witch, Kathrynna, who made a magical trunk and asked him to live there so that he could teach the ways of the good witches to the people of the future. He looked at Jeramie and said, "…and that's how I got here. That big thump was my trunk re-appearing in this attic after 1,000 years."

"Wow! That's a super story. But can you do magic?" inquired Jeramie.

"But of course! I can do anything I wish!" Cerberus beamed.

"Excellent! A real magician," Jeramie said to Max.

"No, I'm not a magician. I am a gnome," corrected Cerberus.

"I don't understand. What's a gnome?" Jeramie looked puzzled.

"You know, gnome — a dwarf, an elf, a miniature fairy, a mythical small person, a short wizard, a gnome," he explained.

"Ohhh...I understand." Jeramie understood, but Max was still confused. "You said your job is to teach people about good witches and their magic, and all that...what people?" asked Jeramie.

"Well...people who deserve to know about things like that," said Cerberus.

"How can you tell?" questioned Jeramie.

Cerberus scratched his wrinkled forehead and pondered the question for a moment, muttering, "...good point, very good point...Well, you need someone who is nice." Jeramie smiled his best Sunday smile. "Umm...hmmm," hummed Cerberus. "Someone who is brave!" Jeramie stood in his best 'knights of the round table' pose. "Yes, yes," uttered Cerberus under his breath, thinking hard. "Someone who is honest and kind to his friends." Jeramie beamed, picking up Max and petting him a little too obviously. "Hmmm," replied Cerberus. "And, Cerberus, someone who wants to learn your magic! Like...well...me!" Jeramie insisted.

"YOU?" chuckled Cerberus.

"Oh, yes please! I know I'd make a good student. I'm already a great student in school. I can learn fast, and I won't let you down or make you angry. I promise!" Jeramie was very excited.

Cerberus was laughing. "Well, perhaps you are right! Such youthful enthusiasm, my, my. Well, perhaps we will give you a try. But I have to warn you right now — if you do not believe, you will not learn the secrets to my magic. If you tell anyone about me, I will disappear for another thousand years. If you do something bad or wrong, my magic cannot help you. You must endure the consequences and help yourself."

"Yes, yes, Mr. Cerberus, sir! I promise I will believe. I'll never tell anyone about you, and I'll never do anything bad." Jeramie and Max were very happy. They were going to become students of magic!

Jeramie's mother could be heard calling them down to the supper table. The entire afternoon had flown by, and now it was evening.

"Go now, Jeramie, and return here tomorrow at four, and you shall begin to understand my ways." With that Cerberus hopped back into the trunk and shut the lid. Jeramie and Max scampered down the attic stairs and into the closet, dusting themselves off as they ran to the dinner table.

The day dragged on and on for Jeramie; four o'clock seemed to take forever to arrive. Jeramie rushed home from school as fast as he could. He grabbed Max and ran to the attic. Cerberus was waiting by the trunk, and was glad to see that Jeramie was as enthusiastic as ever.

"Now, Jeramie, we will begin with the first principle — the most important rule about my magic. Answer these questions that I will now ask you," said Cerberus.

"I'll try," said Jeramie.

"What is it that you would most like to have for your birthday?" asked Cerberus.

"Well, I would like to have a new ten-speed bike," replied Jeramie.

"I see, but don't you already have a bike, Jeramie?" Cerberus questioned.

"Yes, but it's only a three-speed and it's ugly," Jeramie said.

"I see," Cerberus said. He seemed to be somewhat disturbed by Jeramie's answers. "Tell me, Jeramie, can you sing?"

"Yes, and I'm pretty good too!" he beamed.

"That's fine. Now tell me this, if I gave you a choice of getting a new ten-speed bike for your birthday or to let you keep your singing voice, which would you prefer?" Cerberus looked sternly at Jeramie. Max was interested by all the questions, but really wanted to see some magic.

"Well, I would take the bike, no doubt about it. Anyone would," said Jeramie.

"Alright, that's fine. I was just checking.
Now I am going to send you on a little trip.
Close your eyes, and hold on to Max." With
a wave of his hand, gold dust flew from his
fingers, and at that Jeramie and Max
vanished.

A flash — then darkness. Instantly the inky
blackness was replaced by swirling, vibrant
colors; seas of blue and red, green splattered
with purple, giant sheets of yellow all
streaked by. Jeramie felt as though he were
on a roller coaster. Max was feeling queasy;
he really didn't care for roller coaster rides.
He wished it would all stop. They shot along
in the swirls of color for a few moments.
Then, in the distance, they saw a horizon.
They began to fall down, down, down.

They saw people in slow motion, passing by on a city street, cars creeping past, airplanes hanging overhead as if suspended. Suddenly the falling stopped. All of the people, cars and airplanes began to move at normal speeds. Max and Jeramie were now standing on the main street of a modern, glistening, brilliant city.

As they walked along the street, Jeramie looked for a telephone to call home, and Max looked for food. The streets were crowded with beautiful people wearing wonderful clothes, driving fabulous cars, and living in exquisite buildings.

"There mustn't be a single poor person in this whole place! Everyone looks so rich!" remarked Jeramie.

Indeed they were. They had everything anyone could ever ask for, or even hope for. This was a place where, if someone wanted something, they just asked and it would be delivered to them. Everything was provided free of charge, and in any amount desired.

Jeramie and Max saw a small park with a playground. There was a boy about Jeramie's age playing in a sandbox with lots of dump trucks and bulldozers. Max trotted over to the sandbox and stood on his hind legs, peering over the edge. The boy looked up and was startled to find a small furry face looking back at him.

"Hey! What's that?" he exclaimed.

"What's what?" Jeramie asked.

"That! Your toy," said the boy.,

"That's not a toy. That's my dog Max. Haven't you ever seen a dog before?" Jeramie kidded the boy.

"No," the boy said flatly. "...a dog?...hmmmm, I wish I could have a dog."

Jeramie and Max were puzzled. The boy seemed to be saying this into the air, and rather loudly too.

"Who are you talking to?" asked Jeramie.

"I'm wishing for a dog," replied the boy.

"Oh," Jeramie said, not wanting to appear stupid.

"I want a dog!" the boy repeated, only much louder.

There was only the silence of the summer afternoon. Jeramie and Max looked on in bewilderment.

"I want a dog now! A black one with droopy ears and a white tail, just like that one!" He pointed at Max while screaming at the sky. Still nothing happened. Finally Jeramie gave in and asked the boy, "Why are you yelling at the sky like that? Is your wish going to appear out of thin air or something?"

"Yes, as a matter of fact it is!" said the boy.

"I don't get it," Jeramie mumbled to Max. Max looked as though he didn't get it either.

"You're not from around here, are you?" asked the boy.

"What makes you think that?" asked Jeramie defensively.

"Well, for one thing, you've got one of those...." He pointed to Max. "I've never seen a dog before, and because of what you're wearing. If you did live around here, you would have wished yourself some better clothes."

"What do you mean 'wished'?" Jeramie scratched his head.

The boy realized that Jeramie knew nothing of their lifestyle, so he explained the entire concept of wishing for anything you want — and getting it.

Jeramie was blown away. "No way! There is no place like that! You're kidding me. You're a liar!"

"I am not! How do you think this playground got here? I asked for it! If you don't believe me, try it. Ask for something — the first thing that pops into your head," challenged the boy.

Jeramie thought for a moment. "Well, I would like a double fudge chocolate ice cream sundae with whipped cream." Jeramie asked, but nothing happened. "See! I knew you were pulling my leg!"

Now it was the boy's turn to be puzzled. Never before had he seen a wish not come true, especially a simple wish like that. "I'm not pulling your leg. Watch! I wish I had a double fudge chocolate ice cream sundae with whipped cream...and a slab of chocolate cake to go with it!" the boy said to the sky. POOF! There it was — a huge, beautiful, mouthwatering, dripping, scrumptious, thick, chocolaty sundae in a frosty silver dish, with a heavenly moist, delicious slice of chocolate cake sitting next to it. Jeramie couldn't believe his eyes. Max was thrilled.

"That's amazing! Super! I can't believe my eyes! Jeramie was beside himself with joy. The boy handed Jeramie the ice cream and cake. Jeramie tasted it to see if it was indeed real. It was the best double fudge chocolate sundae with whipped cream he had ever tasted. Max managed to snatch a mouthful of the cake. He yelped with pleasure. Not only was it real — it was good. "So I guess your wishes don't come true because you're not from around here," reasoned the boy. "Yeah, I guess so..." mumbled Jeramie through a mouthful of chocolate.

The boy, being the spoiled brat that he was, saw his chance and said slyly, "I'll tell you what I'll do. I will give you ten wishes, absolutely anything you want, no matter what, for...your dog." Jeramie froze. He glared at the boy. Violently he spat out the ice cream and said, "No. I wouldn't trade my best friend for all the wishes in the universe, and if you think I would be so low as to sell my dog, you're crazy." Max was surprised and proud. He had never heard Jeramie stand up to anyone before, not even the other kids at home.

"Well, in that case I'll just take him!" Before Jeramie could move, the rotten little brat had snatched up Max. He held him tightly and yelled, "I wish I had a huge fence around this playground, and that you were on the other side!" POOF! There it was.

Jeramie didn't even have time to react. There he stood, blocked by a towering iron fence, unable to rescue his pal. The stupid little monster of a child sat in his sandbox, laughing, clutching poor Max with his chubby fingers. Next, the boy wished for a piece of rope. He tied one end to his sandbox and the other around Max's neck like a leash.

Max was furious. He had never been forced to wear a leash; he was too good a dog to have to wear one. He thrashed about wildly, wriggling his body in every direction, but the rope held. He was caught.

Max lay down on the grass next to the sandbox and started whining. Jeramie sat by the fence pleading with the boy to let the dog go. The boy sat in his sandbox laughing and sifting sand over his chubby legs.

Jeramie realized that this was a situation that required thinking, not brooding and feeling sorry for himself. He put his mind to work. "What could I possibly give the kid that would make him let Max go?" thought Jeramie. He knew the boy could have anything he wanted, but what exactly did "anything" include? It didn't include dogs; there were none in this place. Perhaps the magical wish-granting force couldn't produce dogs, or didn't know how. Maybe it couldn't produce any animals since there didn't seem to be animals anywhere. Jeramie turned to the boy, "Hey, kid!"

"What?" the boy snapped.

"Where are all the birds around here?" Jeramie asked.

"What? What are birds?" the boy asked.

"Oh nothing, never mind."

Jeramie was forming his idea. He was thinking to himself now, "Okay, not animals — these people can't wish for animals. If they could, there would be some around."

Could this mean they can only wish for man-made things? No, because the sand in the sandbox isn't made by man, neither are the trees in the playground. So, maybe only physical things, things you can touch or feel, can be wished for. Non-materials, hmmm.... Jeramie thought about what he could offer the boy that couldn't be wished for.

Jeramie looked down and plucked a long blade of grass from the ground. He placed it between his thumbs, cupping his hands together, and blew through the opening between this thumbs. This produced a quack-like duck sound.

The boy looked up,

"What was that?"

"Nothing," said Jeramie.

"What was it? Tell me!" pressed the boy.

"I will not tell you. You stole my dog. You're a thief. I don't talk to thieves."

Jeramie turned his back to the boy. He blew into his cupped hands once more and made a high-pitched squeak come out of them.

"Let me see! Show me how to do that!" whined the boy.

"Why don't you just wish for it?" teased Jeramie.

"Alright, I will. I wish I could blow into my hands and make weird noises!" he commanded. He folded his hands together and blew into them. Only a dull, hollow sound came out.

"It doesn't work! Show me!" he cried.

"Why should I show you? You're bad tempered, you're loud, you're rude, you're pushy, you're dishonest and mean!" scolded Jeramie.

"So what! I can be anything I want to be! I can have anything I wish to have! And I can do anything I want to do!" taunted the boy.

"Oh, yeah? You can't do this." Jeramie let out a tremendously loud, vibrating warble that sent shivers down the boy's spine. "Oh, please show me how to do that. I'll give you back your dumb dog. Look at him. He doesn't want to play. He just lies there like a brick and whines. He won't eat, he won't run, he won't even bark. What good is he? I want to be able to make noises like you can!" the boy pleaded.

"Do you promise to keep your word and not try to take him back after I show you how to whistle?" Jeramie asked.

"Yes, I do! Here, here he is." He untied the rope around Max's neck. Max jumped up and shook his fur back into place. He frollicked for a second and then ran to Jeramie. "I'll even take the fence away. I wish this fence would disappear." The fence vanished. Max jumped into Jeramie's arms, growling and barking happily.

"There! Now show me how to do that grass trick!" the boy said. For the rest of the afternoon Jeramie explained to the boy how to position the grass between both thumbs, and how to press them together in certain ways to get different sounds. By late afternoon the boy had almost mastered the art of whistling through grass. Jeramie realized they had to get home for supper.

"Why don't you stay here and have supper with me?" asked the boy. "You can even...."

"I know, I know," interrupted Jeramie, "...we can have whatever we want. No thanks!" Jeramie laughed. He waved goodbye to the boy who was still sitting in his sandbox trying to get various sounds out of a blade of grass.

Jeramie and Max made their way out of the park and back onto the street full of the same beautiful people, cars and buildings. Jeramie walked along, carrying Max, and realized, "You know, Max, we're lucky — we don't have everything we ever wanted, but we have a lot more than we think we do."

At that moment, they were picked up by an invisible force. Once again they were engulfed by all the colors of the rainbow as they made their journey back to the attic of their home.

When they stopped falling, they were standing before the old trunk. Cerberus was waiting there, smiling. "Well, my boy, how did you enjoy your trip?"

"Well, it was okay," said Jeramie.

"Did you learn anything?" probed Cerberus.

"I think so," said Jeramie. "I learned that all the possessions in the world can't buy happiness."

"Well, young man, I think you did learn something today. Now tell me, are you prepared to go further in your lessons?" questioned Cerberus.

"Definitely! Max and I are ready. But I have one small question. Where was that place you just sent us to?" asked Jeramie.

"It's a place where people have been overcome by their own greed," said Cerberus sadly.

"Oh, well. I didn't enjoy that place," Jeramie said with a frown.

"No, but you learned a lesson, and there are many other places you can visit," warned Cerberus.

Max beamed and thought, "I can hardly wait!"